# This book
# belongs to:

..................

..................

For Alex
C.C.

For my beautiful little moo,
Natasha Kitty, with love xxx
J.McC.

Reading Consultant: Prue Goodwin, Lecturer in literacy and children's books

ORCHARD BOOKS
338 Euston Road, London NW1 3BH
*Orchard Books Australia*
Hachette Children's Books
Level 17/207 Kent Street, Sydney NSW 2000

First published in 2011 by Orchard Books
First paperback publication in 2012

Text © Catherine Coe 2011
Illustrations © Jan McCafferty 2011

ISBN 978 1 40830 685 7 (hardback)
ISBN 978 1 40830 693 2 (paperback)

The rights of Catherine Coe to be identified as the author and
Jan McCafferty to be identified as the illustrator of this work
have been asserted by them in accordance with the
Copyright, Designs and Patents Act, 1988.

1 3 5 7 9 10 8 6 4 2 (hardback)
1 3 5 7 9 10 8 6 4 2 (paperback)

Printed in China

Orchard Books is a division of Hachette Children's Books,
an Hachette UK company.

www.hachette.co.uk

# Horse Horror

**Written by**
**Catherine Coe**

**Illustrated by**
**Jan McCafferty**

ORCHARD

Casper the Kid Cowboy loved his horse more than anything else. Blue was always loyal and friendly.

They went *everywhere* together.

To the park . . .

To the shops . . .

Sometimes even to bed . . .

Casper's best friend, Pete, usually came along too. His horse was called Funny Fool. Pete loved Funny Fool, but sometimes he had a mind of his own.

Whoa there! Stop, boy!

Casper and Pete agreed that
everything was more fun with
their horses.

Today, Casper and Pete were
planning a day out. They had
packed a tasty picnic.

The two cowboys were looking
forward to having fun riding
across the desert plains.

But Casper's horse wouldn't
move.

Come on,
Blue!

"What's the matter, Blue?"
Casper asked. It seemed
his horse didn't want to go
anywhere today.

"We'll have to go without him," Pete decided. "It's OK, partner. You can ride up here with me."

Casper was sad. It wouldn't be fun without Blue!

"Let's go this way," Casper said.
"No, let's go that way!" Pete replied.
Funny Fool was confused!

At last the cowboys agreed
to ride west. But Funny Fool
didn't want to go that way.
Instead, he set off towards the
mountains in the east.

"Whoa there!" Pete said to
his horse.
But Funny Fool had made up
his mind. He galloped . . . and
galloped . . . and galloped . . .

Soon they were at the top of
a mountain!

"If Blue was here, I don't think we would have gone the wrong way," Casper said. He sighed. "Let's eat our picnic."

But Casper didn't feel very hungry.

Pete didn't want to eat much either. He was afraid of heights!

It was lucky that the two cowboys weren't hungry. Before they could start eating, Funny Fool had stolen their lunch!

Then they heard a rumbling noise. Casper realised there was a storm coming. Soon it was pouring with rain!

"Can we go home now?" said Pete, shivering.

"Yes, please!" Casper cried. He was desperate to see Blue. It hadn't been any fun without him! The soggy friends jumped onto Funny Fool.

**Home, boy!**

But Pete's horse wasn't ready to go home. He wouldn't move! There was nothing else for it. Casper jumped off and pushed.

Finally, they arrived at Casper's
ranch. Pete ran over to Blue.
He still looked unhappy.
"What's wrong with him?"
Casper asked his best friend.

"Maybe he's tired?" Pete wondered. But Blue didn't look tired. "Cold?" Pete guessed. But Blue didn't look cold.

"Why don't you examine him?" Pete said. "Start at the bottom."

Very slowly, Casper moved
towards Blue's bottom.

"Not *that* bottom!" Pete laughed.
"At the bottom – his feet!"

Casper moved away from Blue's bottom *very* quickly. He looked at his hooves instead.

"You're right!" Casper said. Blue's hooves looked sore and swollen.

**He needs new horseshoes!**

As soon as Blue had new shoes, he was like a new horse. It was amazing.

"Yee-ha!" the cowboys shouted,
as Blue trotted round and
round. Casper's horse looked
so happy!

As the sun set, Pete smiled at his best friend. He had been silly to think they could have fun without Blue.

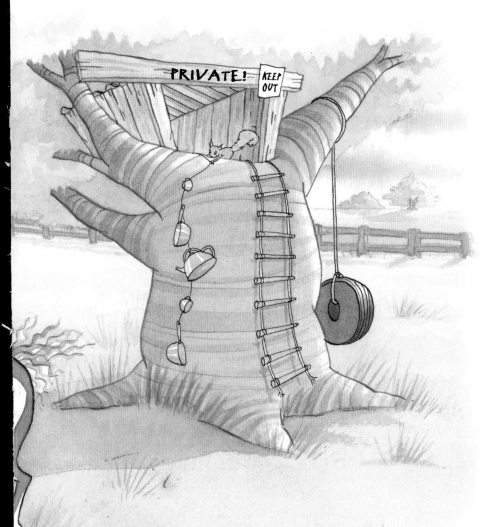

And having fun was what they
did best!

**Written by**
**Catherine Coe**

**Illustrated by**
**Jan McCafferty**

All priced at £8.99

Orchard Books are available from all good bookshops,
or can be ordered from our website: www.orchardbooks.co.uk,
or telephone 01235 827702, or fax 01235 827703.

Prices and availability are subject to change.